# POSSUM CREEK'S BIG FLOOD

THIS BOOK BELONGS TO

For Amie Beth:
the smallest, but not the least

# Possum Creek's Big Flood

Poems by Dan Vallely

Illustrated by Yvonne Perrin

Woollahra

Rain had fallen for a week
On the town of Possum Creek,
As good a fall as most had ever seen.
As it poured and pelted down
The bush, so dry and brown,
Was transformed into a lush and pleasant green.

Seven days and still no sign
That the weather would turn fine,
The dam up in the hills was filling fast.
Old Professor Cockatoo
Was a worried bird it's true,
For he feared the ancient structure might not last.

A wallaby named Clive
Kindly loaned his four wheeled drive
To transport a team to check upon the site.
They took shovels, picks and rope,
Towels, billycans and soap
And urgently departed at first light.

In an hour they were there,
Gazing up in great despair,
It was plain disaster stared them in the face.
There were cracks a metre wide
Up and down and side to side,
They had little time to exit from the place.

Back down the mountain track
Past a boundary rider's shack
Sped the volunteers as fast as they could go.
Over rocks and over stumps
They made four tremendous jumps;
It was life or death — no time for driving slow.

CLIVE

FIRE STATION
CREEK

Into Possum Creek they roared
In that ancient, battered Ford
To the firehouse to ring the danger bell.
As the tension quickly mounted
The assembled crowd was counted,
Everyone was there as far as they could tell.

Just then a rumbling sound
Shook the sodden muddy ground.
It was clear to all the dam had given way
They had seconds to decide —
Should they run, or should they hide?
For a peril great was facing them that day.

Tim Koala in his tree
Said, "My friends it seems to me
That if we stay we'll perish, there is no doubt.
There's a houseboat on the lake
Owned by Sammy Tiger Snake
And I think she's strong enough to ride it out."

Aboard the trusty craft
Creatures trembled fore and aft
As a wall of water twenty metres high,
A tidal wave indeed,
Bore down with frightening speed.
So big it almost blotted out the sky.

Then up and up they rose
Past a flock of startled crows.
The boat was spun around just like a top.
All the animals were sick
And a kangaroo named Mick
Was so upset he couldn't even hop.

Petrified with fright
They clung with all their might
As the raging torrent thundered o'er the land.
The destruction was immense
Every building, shed and fence
Was swept away just like a grain of sand.

Their hopes began to grow
As the boat began to slow,
A bump and they were high and dry once more.
They were sitting on the crest
Of a hill directly west,
Three kilometres from home or maybe four.

What they found on their return
Gave them cause for great concern,
There was nothing left but one big empty space.
Just a bathtub in a tree
Where the township used to be.
Dear old Possum Creek had vanished from the place.

Despite what had occurred
Every animal and bird
Led by Ed Galah and Big Red Kangaroo,
Took hammer, saw and nail,
Fencing wire, log and rail
And rebuilt the town of Possum Creek anew.

Now the tourists flocked to see
That old bathtub in the tree
And to marvel as a platypus in rhyme
Recalls that fateful day
When the town was washed away
And that tidal wave gets bigger every time!

The
End

Other titles in this series:

Possum One The Outback Rocketship
The Great Possum Creek Bush Fire
Professor Cockatoo's Amazing Weatherdust
The Great Possum Creek Earthquake
The Lost World of Possum Creek
The Great Possum Creek Drought
The Possum Creek Olympics

Also illustrated by Yvonne Perrin:

Australian Poems to read to the very young
Banjo Paterson's Animals Noah Forgot